THEY ALSO
Serve

THEY ALSO
Serve
Donald E. Westlake

ÆGYPAN PRESS

This story first appeared in the September, 1961, issue of *Analog Science Fact & Fiction*.

Special thanks to Greg Weeks, Barbara Tozier, and the Online Distributed Proofreading Team (which can be found at http://www.pgdp.net).

They Also Serve
A publication of
ÆGYPAN PRESS

www.aegypan.com

Why should people hate vultures? After all, a vulture never kills anyone...

The launch carrying the mail, supplies and replacements eased slowly in toward the base, keeping the bulk of the Moon between itself and Earth. Captain Ebor, seated at the controls, guided the ship to the rocky uneven ground with the easy carelessness of long practice, then cut the drive, got to his walking tentacles, and stretched. Donning his spacesuit, he left the ship to go over to the dome and meet Darquelnoy, the base commander.

An open ground-car was waiting for him beside the ship. The driver, encased in his spacesuit, crossed tentacles in a sloppy salute, and

Ebor returned the gesture quite as sloppily. Here on the periphery, cast formalities were all but dispensed with.

Ebor stood for a moment and watched the unloading. The cargo crew, used to working in spacesuits, had one truck already half full. The replacements, unused to spacesuits and, in addition, awed and a bit startled by the bleakness of this satellite, were moving awkwardly down the ramp.

Satisfied that the unloading was proceeding smoothly, Ebor climbed aboard the groundcar, awkward in his suit, and settled back heavily in the seat to try to get used to gravity again. The gravity of this Moon was slight, of course — barely one-sixth the gravity of the Home World or most of the colonies — but it still took getting used to, after a long trip in free-fall.

The driver sat at the controls, and the car jerked into motion. Ebor, looking up, noticed for the first time that the dome wasn't there anymore. The main dome, housing the staff and equipment of the base, just wasn't there.

And the driver, he now saw, was aiming the car toward the nearby crater wall. Extending two of his eyes till they almost touched the face-plate of his helmet, he could see activity at the base of the crater wall, and what looked like an air-lock entrance. He wondered what had caused the change, which had obviously been done at top speed. The last time he'd been here, not very long ago, the dome had still been intact, and there had been no hint of any impending move underground.

The driver steered the car into the open air lock, and they waited until the first cargo truck had lumbered in after them. Then the outer door closed, the pumps were turned on, and in a minute the red light flashed over the inner door. Ebor removed the spacesuit gratefully, left it in the car, and walked clumsily through the inner door into the new base.

A good job had been done on it, for all the speed. Rooms and corridors has been melted out of the rock, the floors had been carpeted, the walls painted, and the ceiling lined with light panels. All of the furnishings had been transferred here from the original dome, and the result looked, on the whole, quite livable. As livable as the dome had been, at least.

But the base commander, Darquelnoy, waiting for his old friend Ebor near the inner door of the lock, looked anything but happy with the arrangement. At Ebor's entrance he raised a limp tentacle in weary greeting and said, "Come in, my friend, come in. Tell me the new jokes from home. I could use some cheering up."

"None worth telling," said Ebor. He looked around. "What's happened here?" he asked. "Why've you gone underground? Why do you need cheering up?"

Darquelnoy clicked his eyes in despair. "Those *things!*" he cried. "Those annoying little creatures on that blasted planet up there!"

Ebor repressed an amused ripple. He knew Darquelnoy well enough to know that the commander invariably overstated things. "What've they been up to, Dar?" he asked.

"Come on, you can tell me over a hot cup of restno."

"I've been practically living on the stuff for the last two dren," said Darquelnoy hopelessly. "Well, I suppose another cup won't kill me. Come on to my quarters."

"I've worked up a fine thirst on the trip," Ebor told him.

The two walked down the long corridor together and Ebor said, "Well? What happened?"

"They came here," Darquelnoy told him simply. At Ebor's shocked look, he rippled in wan amusement and said, "Oh, it wasn't as bad as it might have been, I suppose. It was just that we had to rush around so frantically, unloading and dismantling the dome, getting this place ready —"

"What do you mean, they *came* here?" demanded Ebor.

"They are absolutely the worst creatures for secrecy in the entire galaxy!" exclaimed Darquelnoy in irritation. "Absolutely the worst."

"Then you've picked up at least one of their habits," Ebor told him. "Now stop talking in circles and tell me what happened."

"They built a spaceship, is the long and the short of it," Darquelnoy answered.

Ebor stopped in astonishment. "No!"

"Don't tell me no!" cried Darquelnoy. "I *saw* it!" He was obviously at his wit's end.

"It's unbelievable," said Ebor.

"I know," said Darquelnoy. He led the way into his quarters, motioned Ebor to a perch, and rang for his orderly. "It was just a little remote-controlled apparatus, of course," he said. "The fledgling attempt, you know. But it circled this Moon here, busily taking pictures, and went right back to the planet again, giving us all a terrible fright. There hadn't been the slightest indication they were planning anything *that* spectacular."

"None?" asked Ebor. "Not a hint?"

"Oh, they've been boasting about doing some such thing for ages," Darquelnoy told him. "But there was never any indication that they were finally serious about it. They have all sorts of military secrecy, of course, and so you never know a thing is going to happen until it does."

"Did they get a picture of the dome?"

"Thankfully, no. And before they had a chance to try again, I whipped everything underground."

"It must have been hectic," Ebor said sympathetically.

"It was," said Darquelnoy simply.

The orderly entered. Darquelnoy told him, "Two restno," and he left again.

"I can't imagine them making a spaceship," said Ebor thoughtfully. "I would have thought they'd have blown themselves up long before reaching that stage."

"I would have thought so, too," said Darquelnoy. "But there it is. At the moment, they've divided themselves into two camps — generally speaking, that is — and the two sides are trying like mad to outdo each other in everything. As a part of it, they're shooting all sorts of rubbish into space and crowing every time a piece of the other side's rubbish malfunctions."

"They could go on that way indefinitely," said Ebor.

"I know," said Darquelnoy gloomily. "And here we sit."

Ebor nodded, studying his friend. "You don't suppose this is all a waste of time, do you?" he asked, after a minute.

Darquelnoy shook a tentacle in negation. "Not at all, not at all. They'll get around to it, sooner or later. They're still boasting themselves into the proper frame of mind, that's all."

Ebor rippled in sympathetic amusement. "I imagine you sometimes wish you could give them a little prodding in the right direction," he said.

Darquelnoy fluttered his tentacles in horror, crying, "Don't even *think* of such a thing!"

"I know, I know," said Ebor hastily. "The laws —"

"Never mind the laws," snapped Darquelnoy. "I'm not even thinking about the laws. Frankly, if it would do any good, I might even consider breaking one or two of the laws, and the devil with my conditioning."

"You *are* upset," said Ebor at that.

"But if we were to interfere with those creatures up there," continued Darquelnoy, "interfere with them in any way at all, it would be absolutely disastrous."

The orderly returned at that point, with two steaming cups of restno. Darquelnoy and Ebor accepted the cups and the orderly left, making a sloppy tentacle-cross salute, which the two ignored.

"*I* wasn't talking necessarily about attacking them, you know," said Ebor, returning to the subject.

"Neither was I," Darquelnoy told him. "We wouldn't have to attack them. All we would have to do is let them know we're here. Not even *why* we're here, just the simple fact of our presence. That would be enough. *They* would attack us."

Ebor extended his eyes in surprise. "As vicious as all that?"

"Chilling," Darquelnoy told him. "Absolutely chilling."

"Then I'm surprised they haven't blown themselves to pieces long before this."

"Oh, well," said Darquelnoy, "you see, they're cowards, too. They have to boast and brag and shout a while before they finally get to clawing and biting at one another."

Ebor waved a tentacle. "Don't make it so vivid."

"Sorry," apologized Darquelnoy. He drained his cup of restno. "Out here," he said, "living next door to the little beasts day after day, one begins to lose one's sensibilities."

"It has been a long time," agreed Ebor.

"Longer than we had originally anticipated," Darquelnoy said frankly. "We've been ready to move in for I don't know how long. And instead we just sit here and wait. Which isn't good for morale, either."

"No, I don't imagine it is."

"There's already a theory among some of the workmen that the blow-up just isn't going to happen, ever. And since that ship went circling by, of course, morale has hit a new low."

"It would have been nasty if they'd spotted you," said Ebor.

"Nasty?" echoed Darquelnoy. "Catastrophic, you mean. All that crowd up there needs is an enemy, and it doesn't much matter to them who that enemy is. If they were to suspect that we were here, they'd forget their own little squabbles at once and start killing us instead. And that, of course, would mean that they'd be united, for the first time in their history, and who knows how long it would take them before they'd get back to killing one another again."

"Well," said Ebor, "you're underground now. And it can't possibly take them *too* much longer."

"One wouldn't think so," agreed Darquelnoy. "In a way," he added, "that spaceship was a hopeful sign. It means that they'll be sending a manned ship along pretty soon, and that should do the trick. As soon as one side has a base on the Moon, the other side is bound to get things started."

"A relief for you, eh?" said Ebor.

"You know," said Darquelnoy thoughtfully, "I can't help thinking I was born in the wrong age. All this scrabbling around, searching everywhere for suitable planets. Back when the Universe was younger, there were lots and lots of planets to colonize. Now the old problem of half-life is taking its toll, and we can't even hope to keep up with the birth rate anymore. If it weren't for the occasional planets like that one up there, I don't know what we'd do."

"Don't worry," Ebor told him. "They'll have their atomic war pretty soon, and leave us a nice high-radiation planet to colonize."

"I certainly hope it's soon," said Darquelnoy. "This waiting gets on one's nerves." He rang for the orderly.

The End

CPSIA information can be obtained at www.ICGtesting.com
Printed in the USA
BVOW021106161011
273738BV00003B/28/P